For Justin and Hugh
Our Devoted Spouses

This Book belongs to
Jane, Cassandra and

ISBN: 979 8 9883723 2 5
Text Copyright © 2025 Christine West
Illustrations Copyright © 2025 Lizzie Nelson
Published by Lizzie Nelson

Book Cover and Illustrations by Lizzie Nelson

WISDOM

AND

WORLDLINESS

AN AMUSING COLLECTION OF JANE AUSTEN'S IMAGINED
LOST LETTERS, DELIGHTFULLY ILLUSTRATED AND CURATED
INTO A CHARMING SCRAPBOOK

BY CHRISTINE WEST AND LIZZIE NELSON

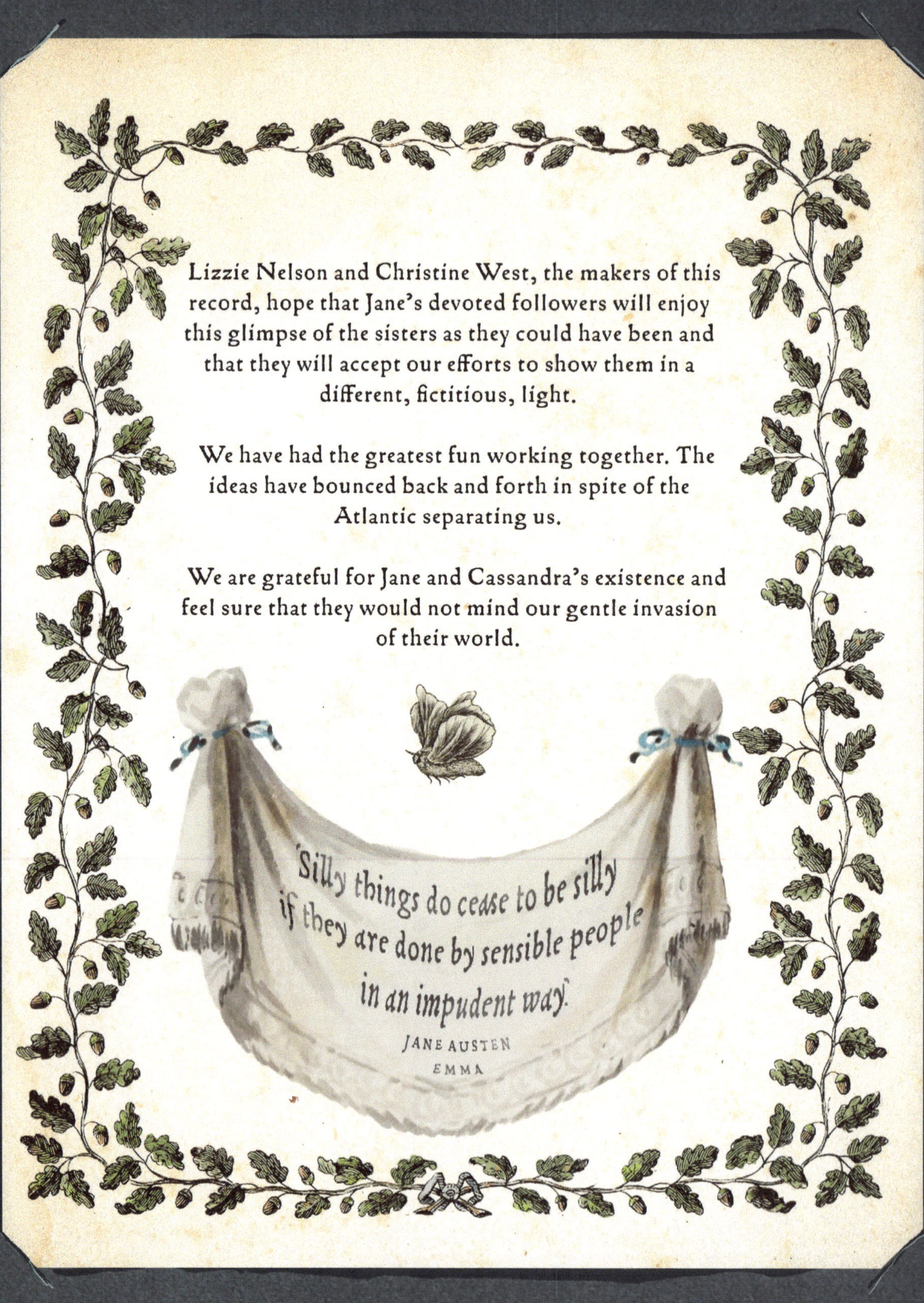

Lizzie Nelson and Christine West, the makers of this record, hope that Jane's devoted followers will enjoy this glimpse of the sisters as they could have been and that they will accept our efforts to show them in a different, fictitious, light.

We have had the greatest fun working together. The ideas have bounced back and forth in spite of the Atlantic separating us.

We are grateful for Jane and Cassandra's existence and feel sure that they would not mind our gentle invasion of their world.

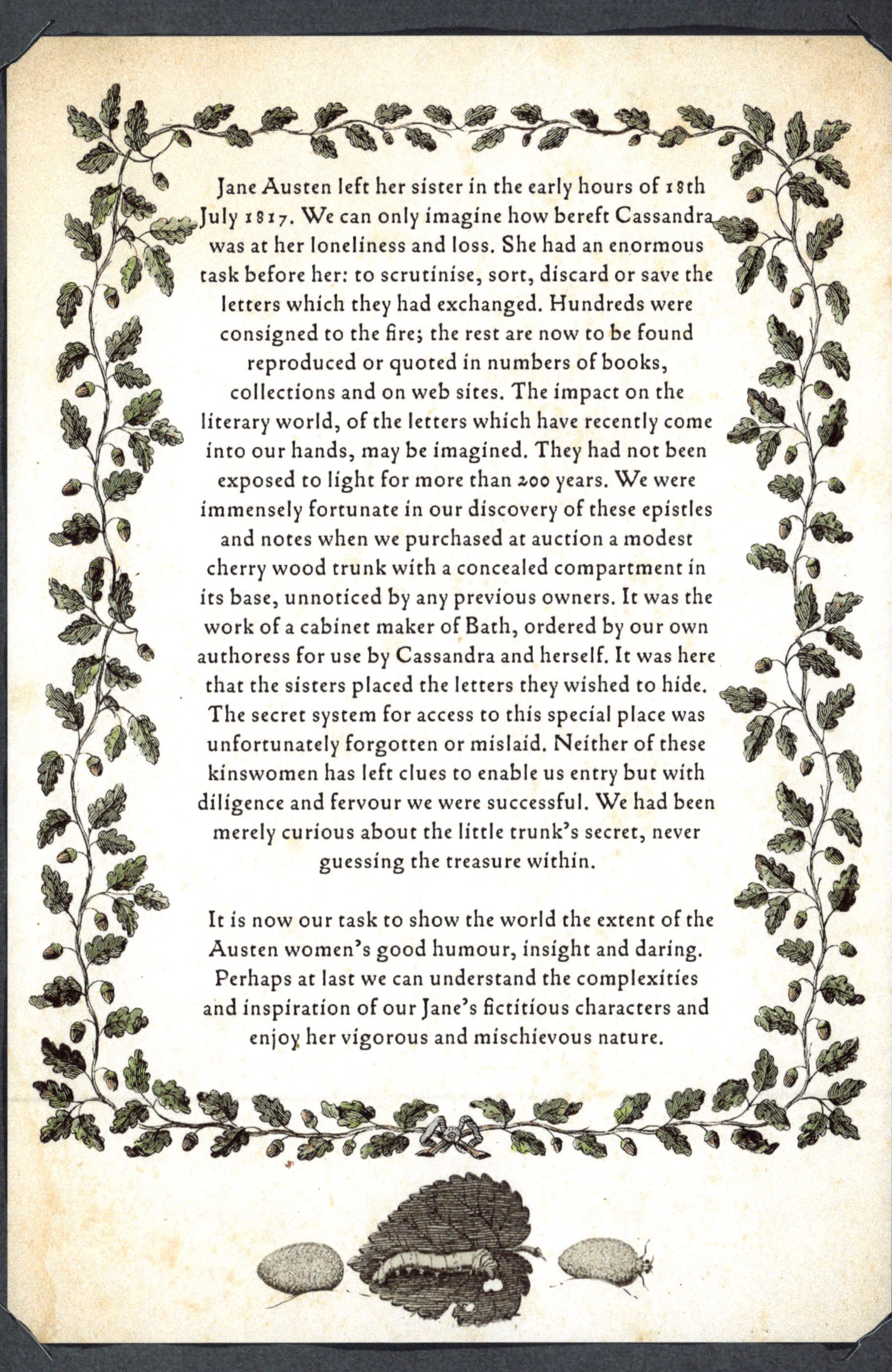

Jane Austen left her sister in the early hours of 18th July 1817. We can only imagine how bereft Cassandra was at her loneliness and loss. She had an enormous task before her: to scrutinise, sort, discard or save the letters which they had exchanged. Hundreds were consigned to the fire; the rest are now to be found reproduced or quoted in numbers of books, collections and on web sites. The impact on the literary world, of the letters which have recently come into our hands, may be imagined. They had not been exposed to light for more than 200 years. We were immensely fortunate in our discovery of these epistles and notes when we purchased at auction a modest cherry wood trunk with a concealed compartment in its base, unnoticed by any previous owners. It was the work of a cabinet maker of Bath, ordered by our own authoress for use by Cassandra and herself. It was here that the sisters placed the letters they wished to hide. The secret system for access to this special place was unfortunately forgotten or mislaid. Neither of these kinswomen has left clues to enable us entry but with diligence and fervour we were successful. We had been merely curious about the little trunk's secret, never guessing the treasure within.

It is now our task to show the world the extent of the Austen women's good humour, insight and daring. Perhaps at last we can understand the complexities and inspiration of our Jane's fictitious characters and enjoy her vigorous and mischievous nature.

In your absence, dear Sister, I have been considering the question of our letters and the possibility of their discovery. I feel certain that Mama would not invade our privacy by reading our correspondence but I am nervous. Might Biddy, although the most reliable of servants, be tempted by the prospect of a little scandal should she happen upon them? I am reluctant to lock everything away — that would embarrass us both — therefore I have devised a delicious plan which should go a good way to solving the problem. I will explain. I intend to seek out a reputable furniture maker. Bath must surely have a number of these — the quality of house interiors I have seen here are proof. I will give instructions for a trunk to be constructed with a hidden compartment in its base. The secret to its unfastening will be known only to we two — and of course to the maker! There we may safely store our most private correspondence. You must on no account forget the procedure for access to the compartment. I hope you approve of my scheme and will advise me upon the choice of wood to be used. Mahogany or walnut?

No one but the writer herself knows whence inspiration comes. My own muse is constantly prompting me to action. Indeed, I have little time to fulfil my role as sister, daughter, good neighbour. I wish only for enough hours at my beloved Desk to express the ideas that enter my mind on catching a smile pass across a face, noticed only by me. I have been known to leave the dining table and mount swiftly to my room to write – and I wish never to stop. My quill and paper are always about my person. My travelling Desk accompanies me everywhere.

La! Biddy says there may be treacle pudding tonight! I am half agony, half hope! (Oh, that's rather good! I might save that phrase for a languishing lover!). You know, better than the rest of the world, of my love for treacle pudding, especially when served with Cook's white sauce. My newest character, Isabella, might in chapter 12 of my new novel, Wisdom and Worldliness, be heard to tell in the most extravagant terms how she looks forward to that agreeable Fare. I confess that I am highly pleased with Isabella, so long as she continues thus to express commonplaces. As for the treacle pudding, do you not wish that you were home?! I shall enjoy it for both of us. Let us hope that we may always have syrup and butter enough to indulge our appetite for sweetness. Such is the importance of small pleasures!

TO A TREACLE PUDDING

My beating heart will not be still.
Only hear them, if you will:
the sounds of preparation
made by good Cook at her station.
La! There will be upon our table,
as splendid as she is able
to concoct, a steamed delight
to set before our Family this night,
crowned with treacle, rich and gold
as any trove in Pirate's hold.

My belief in the wisdom of an ever-present
God has been in doubt this Spring due to the
arrival in our parish of Mr Dolby. He is to
serve as Curate while our Reverend Whitelock is
adventuring in the Holy Lands. My dear, he is
far too comely, uncommonly so, not to attract
quite inappropriate attention. I have observed
from our family pew that almost every young
(female) Person of this parish under the age of
twenty-five has acquired a sudden religious
fervour. Our Saint Nicholas's was quite
stuffed with new bonnets. I even saw cherries on
one, good enough to pluck and to surreptitiously
eat behind the pages of one's Book of Common
Prayer. Upon the return of Reverend Whitelock
and upon Mr Josiah Dolby's departure our
young ladies will be obliged to once again look
for beauty and charm in the members of our
indigenous Congregation, to dutifully attend to
our priest's sermon on the Reasonableness and
Salutary Effects of Fearing God as Governor and
Judge of the World — or else return to their
search for the Almighty in the fields and forest
which surround us.

You do not need to go to church to find God, he may be found under an
oak tree or on the cliff top or in the swaying barley fields.
Unless, of course, the new vicar is uncommonly handsome.

I did not expect Great Things of Biddy at first. I have given thought to her appearance and willing manner and find her more than tolerable, her only deficiency being her inattention. I have had to ask several times for a clean white Napkin to be laid upon the tray when she brings me my Tea. This afternoon she surprised me with a small Raspberry tart, a favourite, which she had begged of Cook, knowing of my liking for that Fruit and saying by round-about means that she feels I do not eat enough to help my Strength until dinner. As to your concerns regarding the Gin, I can assure you, my dear Sister, that I am measured and prudent of its consumption and often take it with water. A little gin does no harm but helps to loosen the brain — but there is no risk of my becoming 'drunken and ungovernable', as Bishop Thomas Wilson feared of the general Population in 1736. I am far, very far, from that deplorable state.

Although we are taught not to count and compare others' consumption of wine or helps of Pudding, I have observed that no one at our table – invited or otherwise – takes coffee as copiously as do I. Coffee can be my undoing. The water closet is too distant from my writing room for comfort. That it should be situated where it is, is a source of embarrassment to Mama and of great amusement to myself. Nevertheless I am obliged to be prudent about the imbibing of my preferred Beverage. I bless this invention of the Water Closet. It has brought civilised society into the Modern World but an earthenware Chamber pot remains the most convenient of Conveniences.

We are to be received in the next week by Uncle
Henry at Canterbury where it is hoped that you
may join us. I shall have but little time for Play
since I am anxious to put finishing touches – alas
there may be many – to the proofs of my
Manuscript. If I am allowed, I shall keep to my
room until it is done. My place of writing is two
pairs of stairs higher and I have been warned that
refreshment will not be brought hourly to such
an elevated place, the maids being too much occupied
with preparations for the Ball. Therefore, in
arranging my surroundings to my liking I shall be
obliged to include, among the quills, ink wells and
blotters, boxes of water biscuits and some of the sugar
plums which Frank has sent to us from Cadiz.
Should there be room in your trunk dear Cassie
pray bring me a supply of comfits – but do not
think to bring me Pontefract cakes or I shall not
reimburse you a penny for those horrors.

Liquorice and Caraway,
Fennel and Anise
Keep those evil herbs and seeds
Far away from me!

You will remember a number of incidents concerning Eliza Cage whilst we took lessons together as children. Was not our tutor a patient man? Eliza was given to playful Pranks and a reluctance to learn any other than watercolour and petit point. Her snorts of laughter are amusing in a gay and pretty girl but I fear that her days of admiration and approval may not last over to her middle years. I observed Mr Portal remark to his neighbour that modern England is changing. I was fatigued with dancing all evening but Eliza showed no sign of tiring nor of quieting her snorts. Sister, would it not be an experiment to ascertain if such peculiarities would add to the charm of a woman in middle years? I shall try it at dinner tonight! Surely, you shall never be considered dull, if you snort when you laugh? — — Our company for dinner last evening included two charming officers from our local regiment. I felt I was quite amusing to tell the story of how our brother Neddy made an ass of himself on his Grand Tour when he mistook the comments, kindly meant, of a fashionable lady on the Spanish Steps in Rome for the advances of a harlot! I threw in a couple of what I felt would be delightful snorts. I can now tell you that there is a VERY fine line between sounding feminine and hysterically porcine!

I have contrived to organise my morning so that I may observe the road from my window. My desk is so positioned that all Activity which takes place before the front of the house is visible. I am particularly drawn to our new Groom — I need scarcely ask that you keep this information for yourself. It is the best of fortune that we are able, by the change in Papa's Circumstances, to afford a carriage and it follows that we have employed William for its care. You may surmise that I am an admirer of a well-turned leg — but my admiration is reserved for his particular method of encouraging True to the shafts. He is both gentle and firm. Is that not to be admired in a man? He will make a very agreeable spouse for someone of his own order. How much easier life would be for ladies like ourselves were we to be given so simple a choice of husband. Today we are to be driven to dine early as guests of the Cages' house, a prospect which pleases me in two particulars: I intend to inspect Mr Cage's library and to take note of William's progress — as well as his fine figure! I will not pursue this line of thought further only to add that I look forward to being assisted from the carriage by him. Pray do not make hint to anyone of my passing interest — for passing it is. After all, I must amuse myself by whatever means available between writing and meals. It rains and I cannot walk out.

ADDRESS TO SPRING thinking of William

O Spring, newborn upon this day,
make not play with me but stay.
Bring showers if thou so will.
On garden and silvan glade spill
thy loveliness; but grant to me
the precious sight of he
who, about his tasks and daily duty,
in your early sunshine brings me beauty.

I have laid aside my Novel for a moment.
Only imagine, little Henry and Errol have
brought to my Fireside certain words which they
learned while playing near the stables. Perhaps
not surprisingly, these came from our groom
William's shapely lips. I understand some to be
impious, others concerned with the reproduction of
our species. I consider myself not easily shocked
in spite of knowing little of the rougher world but
I dare not communicate their meaning to our
little nephews.

We are fortunate, are we not dearest Cassandra, as a family of genteel birth, to have intercourse with members of our esteemed Aristocracy. It is from these Persons that much may be learned and used in the writing of certain passages in my novels. In order to write well on the gamut of human suffering one may experience torment by a tight corset. I sit at my desk in my best silk dress and am convinced that the rustling of my skirts helps give authenticity to my characters conversation. Lady Mary Kenwick the foolish creation of my imagination in the novel which occupies all of my time at present will be ruined by her Vanity and be obliged to become one of the Disadvantaged. It is whilst sitting by an unlit fire, wearing only my drawers that I am thoroughly conscious of the discomfort of humbler people.

It was a very disappointing ball which I attended last evening. My white satin cap was entirely wasted since Mr Bicton could not attend due to a fall from Righteous. There was no one worth talking to save Emily Cornfield, an indifferent supper was provided and there was a want of chairs. We two, being younger than the major number of dancers and at that foolish unbridled age which requires constant amusement, took several turns around the Room - but at a brisk trot, to the dismay of Nanny, who was watching proceedings with Emily's old governess, and those of age above Forty. Mr Curling took unprecedented action, rising from his seat to watch us before removing his pince-nez and continuing to bore those around him. We were rather to regret the mince pies and Stilton taken before our jog but consumed enough cooling Lemonade water to put us right again.

Should you fancy a turn around the room to relieve the tedium of a formal gathering, add some much needed merriment to the proceedings by doing so at a brisk trot.

I happened to remark on the Treaty of Paris at dinner tonight, and to my horror was firmly slapped down by that pompous Donkey, Lord Petherick and was told that ladies should not offer an opinion on European and indeed World Affairs. I am livid, dear Sister! We must read and read and read, forearmed with the knowledge that the opinions of small men are revealed to be ill informed nonsense. I say, plunge into the arts, into plays and Current Affairs. Read copiously on every subject so that you may briefly shine at luncheons...should you (and I say this literally fuming!) be permitted to speak! Let us find ways to inform ourselves further on matters of politics and beat Lord Petherick at his own game. We will challenge him to a debate on the recent upheaval in France. What do you wager that he will not have read Edmund Burke and His Impact on the British Political, Social and Moral Response During the French Revolution (1790-1797)? Do not groan: I do not expect either of us to read the Burke in its entirety.

THEATRE-ROYAL, BAT[H]

This present THURSDAY, the 18th of Sept[ember]
Will be perform'd a COMEDY, call'd

SHE STOOPS to CONQ[UER]

Or, The MISTAKES of a [NIGHT]
(Written by Dr. GOLDSMI[TH]

You will exclaim at this but I am immersing myself in
the works of Mr Oliver Goldsmith, whose play The Stoops
to Conquer I have long admired in the published version.
I believe that the author fancies himself to be of a
Shakespearean bent as his Plot is complex and full of
amusing Misunderstandings. Though a woman, I feel
more than capable of unravelling the convolutions of his
tale. I fear that Papa would never allow either of us to
attend a Performance at Covent Garden – or farther still
at Wisbech, both towns being too great a distance to attend
without the expense of an Overnight Stay in either.

Thomas, Mr. HASKER,   Fringe, Mrs. DIDIER.
Cudden, Mr. G. SUMMERS.   And Mrs. Cheshire, Mr. ROWBOTHAM.

*** * To begin precisely at Half past SIX o'Clock.**

Boxes 5s.—Pit 2s. 6d.—First Gallery 1s. 6d.—Upper Gallery 1s.

Tickets and Places for the Boxes to be taken at the Box Lobby of the Theatre where Attendance will be
given from Ten to Two and from Three till Five.   Vivant Rex & Regina.

Friday, MUCH ADO ABOUT NOTHING, with POOR VULCAN.
Saturday, the GRECIAN DAUGHTER, with Entertainments.

I was so tempted by the weather this day, after my Airing in the fly which has been graciously lent to us by our Uncle Henry, that I took my small lap desk out into his beautiful gardens here. I have leisure to enjoy the sunshine while writing – although this is occasionally accompanied by a strong breeze. Our groom William, who now serves also as manservant to Papa and accompanies him here, happened to be passing – I must suppose by chance – as a gust of air carried several of my papers across the lawns. I had not need even to rise to chase after them as with a vigorous and manly energy he hastened to gather and bring them to me. This would ordinarily have been a pain in the arse (a word which I learned from splendid William today) but that it brought his male presence most agreeably close. I must contrive to let such small accidents occur again. The occasional cup or handkerchief may need to be sacrificed to that end.

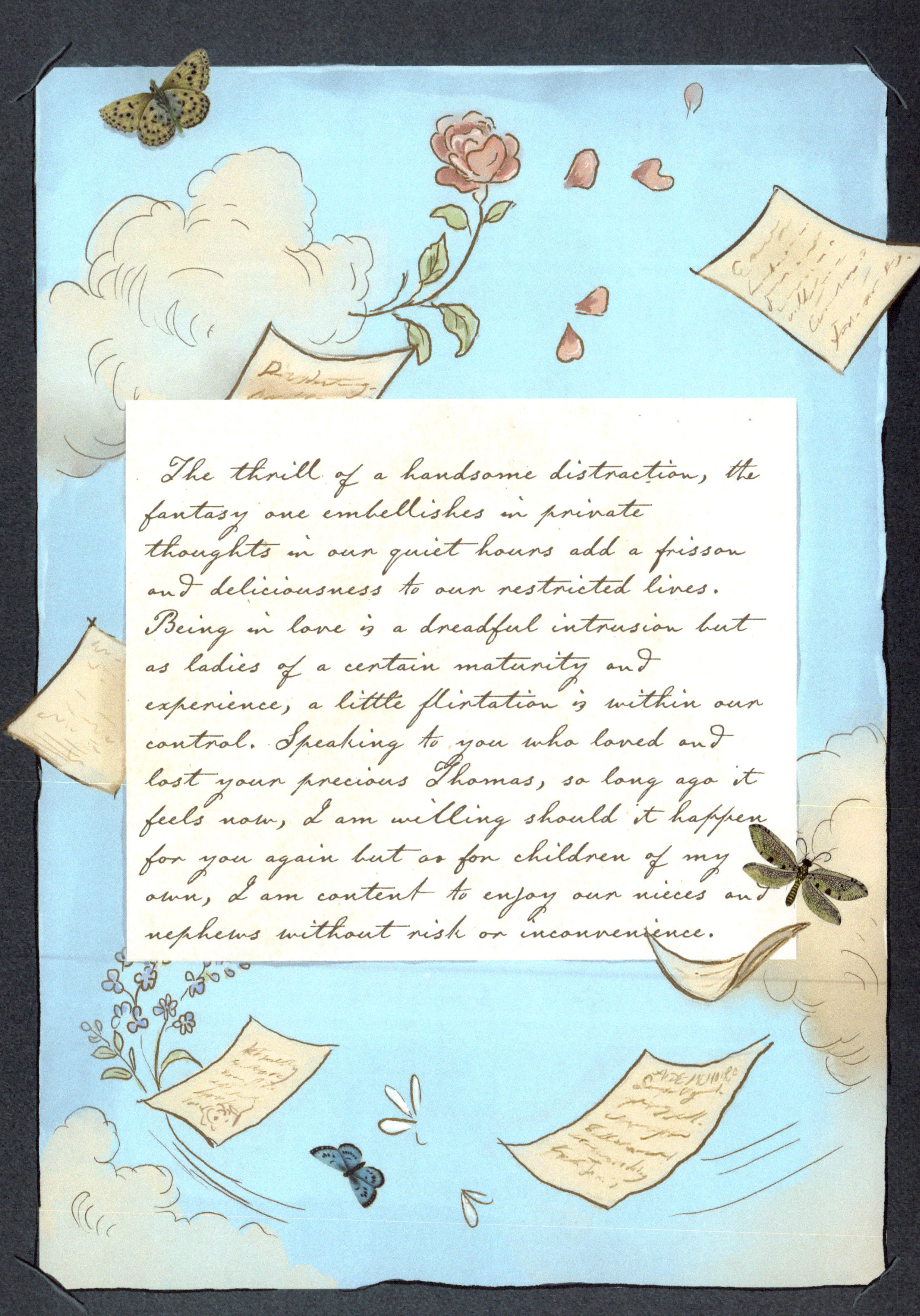

The thrill of a handsome distraction, the fantasy one embellishes in private thoughts in our quiet hours add a frisson and deliciousness to our restricted lives. Being in love is a dreadful intrusion but as ladies of a certain maturity and experience, a little flirtation is within our control. Speaking to you who loved and lost your precious Thomas, so long ago it feels now, I am willing should it happen for you again but as for children of my own, I am content to enjoy our nieces and nephews without risk or inconvenience.

Charles is returned from India bringing the Scorpion home to Portsmouth by way of Malta. We all were given gifts: a silverknife for Henry, sweet wine for Papa and any number of embroidered silk shawls. I covet some peacock feathers but these are to be the property of someone else (you may guess whom!). I would dearly have loved to travel and, perhaps, sailed to the Indies. But best of all to have taken the Grand Tour. I have a longing at times to travel greater distances than to Bath and London but it is fruitless to sigh over the Indies since I could never afford the comfort of so costly a voyage. Indeed, the thought of travelling so far without you beside me, beloved Cassandra, makes me quite faint. I should have no one to whom to complain about the poor service or the weather. I understand however that in warmer climes than those which assail England, one may discard one's second layer of drawers and bodices with impunity. I should become a quite different Jane with no one of our acquaintance near and should discard more than my drawers! Perhaps on reflection it would be prudent to remain here at Chawton and leave others to their Grand Tours.

A Plea to the Scorpion

O gallant galleon heading o'er the sea
bring our dear brother back to port in safety.
Let not misfortune's evil mar our meeting.
May he bring tropics' shine to light our greeting.
But, sweeter still, we, in great anticipation,
hope for silks and wine and spices from that nation
where swing bold monkeys from trees o'er-laden
with exotic fruits, where wild peacocks make display,
where clothing is discarded in the heat of day.

There can be few things worse to endure than
the pain of a broken bone – excepting the birthing
of a child which I shall only know second hand. I
have been obliged to resort to the taking of a deal
of laudanum to ease my discomfort and to help
me forget my inexcusable conduct last Thursday
fortnight. I beg you not to refer to
this after receipt of this letter. You asked what
entered my head to accompany William to gather
mushrooms in the furthest wood. I will
only admit to several occasions when our lips met
and to my foolishly running away from our eager
servant. Now I wish I had kept close – who
knows what I may not have learned instead of
tripping over my cloak and the root of a tree.
The result: a fracture to my ankle and a
liking, nay dependence, upon that little bottle.
You will please to excuse the brevity of this letter.
I must take more. At present I do not
trouble with the bother of spoons for my doses.
Dearest Cassandra, come soon I beg.

As I convalesce I am working on the large piece of embroidery which I began, oh! four years ago? Such ladylike designs bore me to distraction. I was thinking of sewing instead humorous portraits of all the silly people we know onto kerchiefs. What a delight it would be to blow one's nose on Lady Petherick! I am embarking on a series of handkerchiefs. Imagine the deliciousness of such images embroidered on finest Irish lawn. These will afford amusement to the ladies into whose pockets my little works will be secreted. The work of the laundresses, whose task it is to wash them, will be brightened. We might consider selling these since we are so often in want of money. Further, I intend to set aside my profits against future rainy days. Are you familiar with market trading, dear sister? I fear that this means of selling pieces of embroidery and other Articles will fast overtake the country and that loyalty to our local emporia will diminish but I would sell my own precious writing desk before the bailiff should remove Papa's armchair or Mama's cherrywood sewing box. I beg, do not make hint of this little scheme of mine to our Parents.

THE HAPPY COTTAGERS

Tiny Blessings rained upon their leaky roof and filled their happy home.
How Alicia lov'd her fair Frederick, though but the Second Son and a poor Minister.
For does not Love inherit the greatest riches after all?

To be, or is Frederick, without means to improve one's surroundings (I fear that my cousin's chimneys and roof leadings are a cause of much anxiety) is very hard but he is infinitely more lovely, interesting and learned than any Lord S. His wife was this week delivered of a fifth Blessing which I shall soon see. Alicia is fortunate to have escaped the danger of linking her future with Lord S but our Frederick, being of an infinitely greater intellect and beauty than that nobleman, is the better catch. Also, imagine oneself lying beside Lord S — or being lain upon by him! — in his enormous bed. The image is frightful. Alicia has her minister and I believe that Frederick's nightly attentions must make both forget about the roof above their heads.

After writing this letter I shall have no more pleasant news to tell of our groom – although there is a silver lining to this dark cloud as I shall relate. Papa has been obliged to dismiss William, in part because we can no longer afford to keep a carriage and I fear also that rumours have reached him about the Mushrooming incident. William is to serve at Mapleforth House. It is my hope that I may be invited thence by Lady M and shall contrive to do so. This will afford me a glimpse of him on such occasions, a small comfort but a silver lining indeed. My donkey days are now over since advanced age obliges our dear little Trot to retire. She is consigned to bringing small parcels from town. The sight of her in her little leather shoes when she pulls the roller across the grass is delightful. I shall ride Prince and very glad am I to do it – my thighs will benefit! The pity only is that one is obliged to ride sidesaddle. Why may we females not be permitted to dress as do the gentlemen so that our lower limbs may be on show? I can only imagine the light in William's eyes if this were so.

To a Faithful Donkey

O Trot, would that I could restore to thee
those youthful days of our first company!
No gentler, meeker steed could i'er be found
than little Trot who, in her youth, would take
her charges over hilly field and ground
where other finer mounts refused to ride.
Now hers are the days of leisure and pride,
her task no more to bear us but to draw
the cutter and make short the greening sward,
her dainty feet in shoes of leather clad.
Her wise and thoughtful head seems glad
to serve us through the warmest summer days.
We marvel at our dear and sing her praise.

The stables from my
bedroom window with
Trot and Sweet Williams

Since William's removal to a grander situation —
grander in its surroundings certainly — I have
not felt moved to sit at my open window when
writing. Today, however, has brought something
of a change. I am determined to apply myself
only to the plot of my novel. It is fortunate
that my constitution is good and that I have
not so far suffered the fate of many to be
inconvenienced by a running nose or, worse, by any
fever, scarlet or black. For this I thank a
benevolent God and my common sense. I wear a
cashmere shawl at all times. This warms me,
now that sight of William no longer can.

Upon mature reflection I have decided to remain a spinster. Marriage to a man of substance and good health would no doubt be exciting at first and a comfort in the long term but I will not hide from you, dearest Cassandra, my thoughts concerning the marriage bed itself. How often have I pictured in every detail a man such as groom William whose nightly attentions, like those of our cousin Frederick to Alicia, would doubtless have resulted in a prodigious amount of little children. Such a marriage of course could never come about, our difference in rank being the greatest barrier — I would also mention his attraction to every housemaid and general servant. No, I will not surrender my right to the consumption in bed of shortbread, to a kitten or a puppy in the folds of my counterpane nor to ink blots on my nightgown — which shall in all other ways remain unstained.

Consider becoming a spinster; you may accumulate crumbs, kittens, puppies, books, ink and paper in the bed without reproach.

I had a mind at first to name my little white
cat for cousin Lucy. Both young lady and Cat
are such fresh and charming companions but
I fear that confusion - even indignation - may
arise if human Lucy should visit our present
home. I therefore have settled upon Alba for
purposes of calling and for gaining her attention.
She has so far presented us with two litters of
delightful children, many of these masculine
specimens, most of whom are gone from here - I
know not where. Dear Sister, I am here in
Southampton and you are in Godmersham!
At least I have Alba for company.

I was again reminded, as on so many and so frequent occasions, of how indispensable you are to me. I am in need of your assistance in trimming my Pelisse. You would tell me, would you not, if my head dress with Bugle band is fitting for the Ball at Mapleforth this evening? I may even resort to the cap I altered this day which you have not yet seen. I confess that even before appearing in public I have a longing to impress William should he be among those meeting the carriages. If the light of admiration appears in his eye then I know I may enter the House with confidence.

I am conscious, Cassandra, that being the elder of we two daughters you reserve for yourself the privilege of crossing boundaries of behaviour that I would not. For my part, I advise you, in advance of the Ball, not to pinch my cheeks. I am not above striking out in response. The kerfuffle between two sisters in feathers and finery at the top of the Assembly Room staircase would make a memorable sight! However your excuse, that pinching will bring colour to my complexion, is not acceptable as I am perfectly able to do this myself. May I borrow your second best cap, dearest Sister?

A PINCH FOR A PUNCH

Oh do not pinch me Sister Dear, I'll not be nipped today,
I'll not be hauled and pinked about before the Ball, I say.
I'll bite my own lips Berry red, and slap my cheeks to blush
Crimson not from the Assembled gaping, mortifying hush!
Should your meddling not desist, no further shall be said
You see this pin upon my cap? I'll run you in the head.

Perhaps my Love I'm still to meet upon the jouncing floor?
Perhaps it was he did not see the scuffle at the door!
But just as music swelled and spun, a Rake crept up instead
And pinched me where a Maiden sits! I nearly dropp'd with dread.
Oh though I'm gentle when I choose, I'm not so finely bred
So heed me well, both Kin and Knave, ere any hand is spread
I've teeth and nails and pins enough to run you in the head.

You will doubtless unfairly declare, my dear sister, that I am the most indiscreet of souls. This accolade I attribute not to myself but to Miss Penn with whom I walked to Steventon yesterday afternoon. She was quite breathless with news of Mr Cole. I was unaware that he is returned here. Miss Penn has sworn me to utmost secrecy, having related an incident concerning herself and that gentleman. I do not doubt that she has spent weeks – nay, months – sighing over him. I find his presence, shall we say, overwhelming. He occupies one's space so. Indeed, Miss Penn's space was shamefully invaded when he and she were walking and he touched... I must not go on. Mr Cole has turned out to be a Vile Character. His stockings and his general attire leave much to be desired and we must be thankful that – well, I have already said too much. Let it be a lesson to her. One does not, with impunity, walk alone in shady places with such as he, wearing one's lightest clothing.

I intend to carry out research for my writing by exploring the harbour, the slums, the workhouse and inns, taking a small kerchief to put to my nose. I am hopeful that you will return to Mama and me before the month is passed. I am eager to carry out further research for the next chapter of my novel. If I am to write with an authentic pen of Mary Renwick's descent into degradation I must take courage and penetrate the darker areas of our town – even those where Mama does not venture when she takes food and Necessities to our less fortunate neighbours. Will you not take Mama's place and accompany me, dear sister? Such outings cause me to realise that though we ourselves may be disadvantaged by certain circumstances these are as nothing compared to the sufferings of those who inhabit the slums with no chance of escape. I shall be careful to wear my brown calico and gardening boots in order to not make envious those to whom I intend to address myself. I shall take a plentiful supply of kerchiefs and a nosegay of rosemary and you must do the same if you agree to come with me. I fancy we will look charming, though not overly so, in matching caps.

RESEARCH YOUR SUBJECTS: Explore the harbour, the slums, the workhouse. Take a small kerchief to put to your nose.

The Dandizette Maria Doll

I feel that I must write to you, my dear Cassandra without delay since you are expected home from Bristol this very week. Here is a warning. We are at present visited – nay, invaded – by a most unwelcome person, Miss Maria Benson, who arrived here unannounced. She surprised me when in a state of near Undress, to my confusion and her amusement. She was clad in goodness knows how many layers of fashionable flounces and with a deep beaded hem to her dress. I, by contrast, had on only my simple silk with bugle trim (3/4d yd), no cap and my second best slippers. We must be grateful to Mr Arkwright for his improving Water Frame. Cotton muslin is to be had so much cheaper now and I intend ordering a printed length. We will compete as best we may. Miss Benson is to stay for at least 7 days, no doubt with the hope of attracting the attention of a suitor. I beseech you to join with me in out-doing her in our fashions. You have a better selection of fans by far and I shall borrow Mama's best pearls.

My dear Wilfred, It falls to me as second eldest cousin to write to you in utmost seriousness. Allowing that you have suffered so much from recent pressing – and believe me I can imagine the harsh conditions aboard ship for those of low rank – allowing this, I say, as sufficient punishment for the recklessness you have displayed in frequenting docks and ports, I am, even so, disposed to further chastise you for not having communicated your movements to your mother. Your parent was desolate at your enforced departure. My advice to you, lest you should be forgetful in future, is to have her name – MAMA DEAREST – tattooed upon your arm. Please heed this advice, little Cous. Pressgangs are everywhere on our coasts at present and I should dislike to be obliged once again to supply handkerchiefs and smelling salts to your distressed Mama. Resume your studies for the Clergy. You are far too pretty for the company of rough naval men.

Fair Wilfred Unwisely Awaits Adventure

You had better come home and see what new delight is here. I recognise that in past years I have resisted intrusion on my solitude, valuing it as I do, and have put my time to good use in my duties and my writing. I never could have imagined so sweet a nature, so kind a face and so keen a mind to exist in one person — yourself apart. I am speaking of a gentleman called Mr Robert Thorne. He came to inspect Papa's library and assess its worth should our fortunes refuse to come good and selling the only way to improve our lot. He was respectful to Papa and gracious to Mama and me. He visits, I believe, more often than is needed and we have had many exchanges over tea. Yesterday he asked to see the garden and it was to me that this delightful duty fell. Out of sight of the house but discreetly he took my hand and told me he hopes to know me better. Sister, that is all I wish for myself.

AIDE — MÉMOIRE
Ply him with endless cups of tea, for Love
may be found in a teapot-stirred and
steeped and fragrant!

You will not recognise me now. I am quite overwhelmed with fury and dislike for treacherous Maria Benson. She has quite ruined Christmas and driven away Robert Thorne from our house. I cannot endure the rest of this festive season without you, Cassie, but if duty compels you to stay with our cousin and nurse her to good health then I shall be obliged to wear the mask of forbearance behind which no one may see me weep. I cannot help suspecting that he and she are at this moment in each other's company and only wish that my sweet William were still about the place. I should never have looked into Mr Thorne's eyes had he been in attendance.

A MORAL TALE

May all who are on fickle fame and passing fashion bent
Take heed of one such who, having mere beauty as her share,
and throwing aside the rules of good conduct in the Fair
ran headlong to the cruel fate of reckless flirts. She lent
her priceless Self and lost all in vain pursuit of false love.
Take not another's man but from misconduct rise above.

Let us be done with sly pretence. Admit that you
throughout these festive days of mistletoe and yew
in guise of friendship under that pale-berried bough
made false designs upon my love whom until now
was to you nothing, lower than a mere servant.
How much like to yours is the tongue of the serpent!
Be like your heavenly namesake, just and pure of heart -
if not, go! In our revels take no further part.
Be gone with your fine lace and frills of high fashion.
Your shallow flirting cannot outwear our passion.

But wait! To my own ends your falseness I may use
and prove once for all whom 'twixt us my love will choose.

Let us, upon your return from Bristol, attempt to make some sense of our financial situation. Much may be made of our wanton expenditure this season on shoe buckles and fans but our Mama must be spared concern. You will no doubt continue to trim bonnets profitably for our acquaintances and friends while I shall lose myself in the completion of Wisdom and Worldliness. Writing is my greatest pleasure and consolation. Once published, I anticipate acquiring vast quantities of money. Then we shall have new caps and any amount of stockings and marzipan to share.

We are neither of us ready to be old and invited to dances only to chaperone one another. I regret the distance between us in particular at present and heartily wish that I were there to guard you from foolish haste. I must have all news, Cassandra. Do not keep short but write with every detail of your rapprochement to this Captain Tremayne of whom we know nothing. Is he of our County or one nearby? Are we to meet his family if he should make you an offer? If so, consider its consequences. You may be able to imagine your loving actions toward him, and his to you, but have you gone farther in your mind than the orange blossom and the wedding breakfast? Think how delightful the moment when you may at last retire and find each other clad in your complicated nuptial finery: your maid will be downstairs, you will have only Walter's clumsy hands to undress you to your skin – and, most alarming of all, those many brass buttons of his which you will be impatient to unfasten. Without benefit of practise in these matters you may find yourselves still clothed when the early blackbird heralds the dawn of your first day as Mrs Tremayne!

This Pine Apple

Not from a pine do I this Apple pluck
but from my father's glorious Pine house.
Should Dame Fortune reward me with good luck
and grant me fair Cassandra as my spouse
I pledge my honour and my riches to she
who by our first embrace has honoured me.

WJ

Close the book and

A clandestine kiss

My hand in letter writing and Manuscript is not so pretty as yours, sister, nor so neat and small, but it does have the advantage of disguise, being practically illegible. Only persons above the age of five and twenty will have the time and resolve to apply themselves to deciphering my scratching. I exaggerate of course. You are aware that I am perfectly able to write legibly of nothing in particular in order to fill a page for an aunt or other of our relations. Letters between us may conceal all manner of secrets. But leaving aside notions, pelisses and bodices and returning to the question of your Captain (here I shall depart from legibility) what became of the caresses you accepted from him behind the conservatory's largest palm? I am anxious to know the sequel.

There is nothing quite so delicious as a quiet revolt. I was in Hall's Bookshop today and purchased a copy of Francis Grose's Classical Dictionary of the Vulgar Tongue. It is handy when at a loss for words. Also, there is surely no such thing as bad vocabulary. God gave us Free Will, there was no caveat, he did not add, 'But thou shalt not say Bumfiddle,' or such words. My mind is divided now, since you introduced me to this Dictionary. Shall I ever find the courage to introduce 'sugar stick' to Elizabeth B's mind or conversation when she considers the attributes of Mr Darcy — of whom I am very fond? Far from being 'a duke of limbs', tall, awkward and ill-made, he is a very fine fellow and his manliness would not be far from her thoughts (or mine!). I may allow him reference to her 'apple dumplings'. It is tempting to rouse the indignation of my refined readers.

Apple Dumplin Shop. A woman's bosom.
Apple-pye Bed. A bed made apple-pye fashion, like what is called a turnover apple-pye, where the sheets are so doubled as to prevent any one from getting at his length between them: a common trick played by frolicsome country lasses on their sweethearts, male relations, or visitors.
April Fool. Any one imposed on, or sent on a bootless errand, on the first of April; on which day it is the custom among the lower people, children, and servants, by dropping empty papers carefully doubled up, sending persons on absurd messages, and such like contrivances, to impose on every one they can, and then to salute them with the title of April Fool.
Apron String Hold. An estate held by a man during his wife's life.

Aqua

Following your advice, Sister, I will keep the opening phrases of P&P after all. I have hesitated to include this universally acknowledged Truism but it will in any case be quickly forgotten as the reader progresses through the tribulations of Elizabeth B and her suitors. No one could associate my narrative with the trials of our own dear Father. Had most of us been born girls and he still with us, I should not have begun in so obvious a fashion. Further, in writing this novel I take my revenge upon a certain titled neighbour who will surely not recognise herself in the character of Lady Catherine. I think you will agree that it is a wickedly accurate likeness. I heard myself referred to, by her, as Plain but Allowable in her drawing room the other evening! I shall certainly not readily accept further invitations to make up numbers at one of Lady P's gatherings.

I have some news for you which I am eager to communicate. We are to have a new neighbour! We dined with eight others at Mapleforth House last evening. Among the company was a Mr Josiah Pawford, yet another odious character with whom my readers would readily be familiar. These specimens appear throughout the ages. He has taken the Hall which stands within the grounds of the Great House and there is to reside with Mrs Pawford, who I fancy is a mouse of a woman, and their youngest sons. We might have spent the evening very pleasantly but for having our noses snubbed and our fingers rapped by that man whenever any of the party ventured a remark or – heaven forfend – an opinion. Pomposity thy name is Pawford. I care little that he sits at the Assizes to judge we lesser beings. He seems unable to allow a voice other than his own – save, on occasion, that of his hostess – but must trumpet forth his boasts on the subject of Royal Connections and the sovereigns in his purse. He was certainly in liquor but it may be that his behaviour is already forgotten this morn – but not by me or, I am certain, by Lady M.

I consider every person I meet as merely a character study for my next novel. My time here in Bath, alas without you my Sister, and frequent attendance in the Upper Rooms give me ample opportunity to observe those who dance around us. One such creature shall find her way into my next novel, so rouged and stupid was she — her pursuit of her drunken husband afforded us much amusement as the woman's penetrating Voice could be heard in every corner of the room. Before W&W is completed I shall have introduced my readers to them. If read with attention and intelligence they may be able to identify this intent.

PEMBERLEY
PRIDE & PRE

The best of news! I do believe P & P to be a triumph. I am told that it has been published to great acclaim and S & S is printed in a second edition. Since many accolades have reached me I am convinced that writing my manuscripts in Sepia Ink has helped them become immediate classics. Their appearance was not lost on Messrs Crosby or upon Mr Egerton. These Gentlemen have been proven wise in publishing as is demonstrated by both the critical and popular laudation which has come to me. I would rather not address my mind to the creatures which must be sacrificed to the manufacture of my ink. After all, to paraphrase, there must be many more squid in the sea than ever came out of it.

I have resigned myself to happy spinsterhood
and am unlikely ever to marry and bear
children but should fate award me a spouse
and a litter of noisy boys and girls, I should
not allow their clamour to distract me from
my manuscripts. There will in any case be a
battalion of nursemaids and governesses in
place from the birth of the first infant. The
infants may run as wild as they please in
their care whilst I shall close myself up in
the pantry where I may consume quantities of
cake. And wine.

Dear Cassandra, Upon mature thought I have decided to continue to accept summons to dinner or luncheon by Lady Petherick. Her delicious food makes an invitation to her table almost irresistible and there is always the hope that an unattached Gentleman may be one of the party. As a writer I may glean any number of delightful phrases for use in my Novels. On the last occasion chez elle I overheard a guest three places away describe to her neighbour the inordinate amount of Sugar she has acquired since her husband's return from the Indies. I am sure that this excess has contributed to the dulling of her Complexion, if not her mind. I shall endeavour to quell the rebellion I feel and to look about — with the greatest discretion at the male company around me. I have enough charming ribbons and informed topics of conversation at my disposal to seduce the most stubbornly celibate young man — should I wish to.

Here I am, dearest sister, safely ensconced in my writing corner in dear fashionable Bath whilst you are committing acts of folly in Belgravia. No doubt wearing your China Crape contributes greatly to your triumph and I am pleased to hear of the success of your visit. I must know all concerning your dalliance – if dalliance it be – with the attentive Mr Kirkland. I feel that a warning note should be sounded, albeit from your younger sister. Be vigilant where Male hands are concerned, keep your lips turned from those of this dashing Hairdresser. It may be that his close proximity and manner of handling your person, will tempt you to behave unwisely. Let him linger over the dressing of your hair, by all means, it will do no harm to meet him later on equal terms and not while he is hot. I may say that I write with a certain experience, as well as with great affection for you.

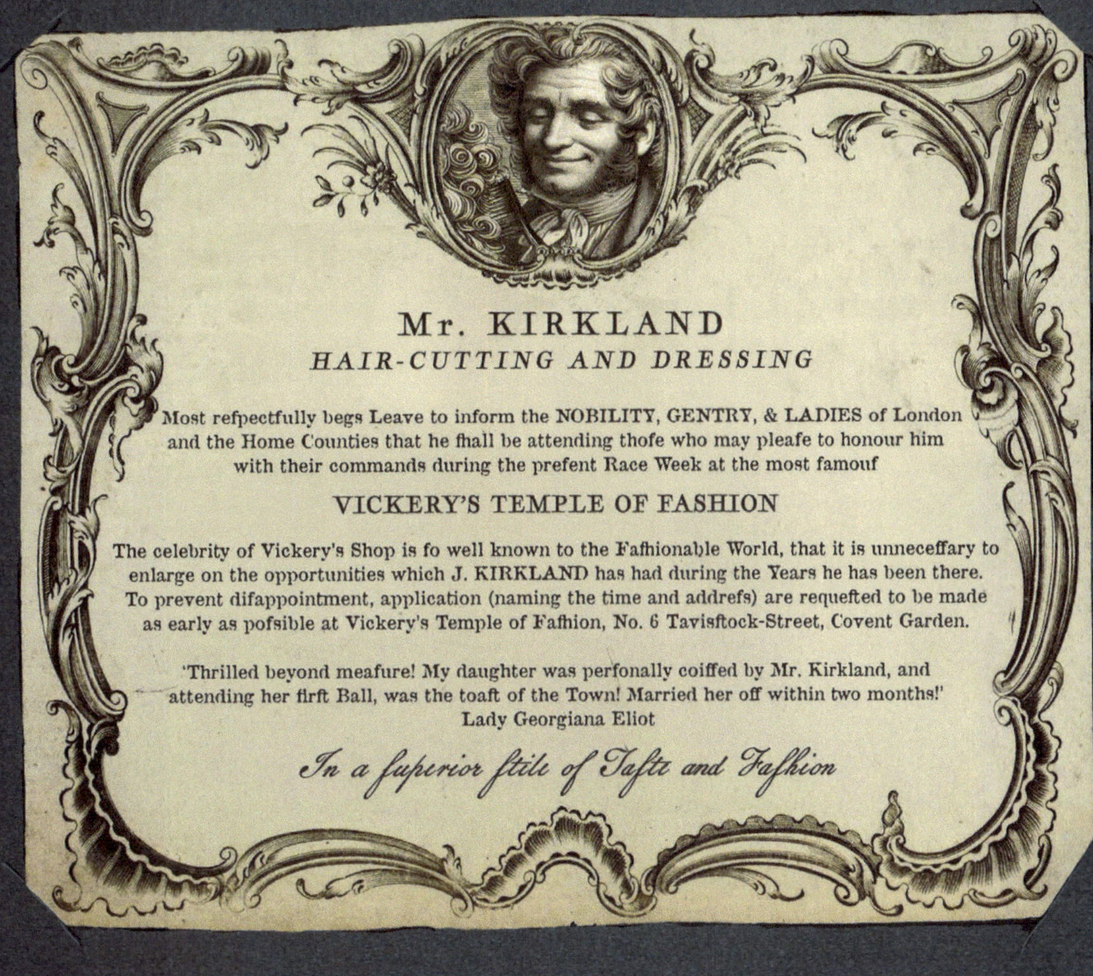

Mr. KIRKLAND

HAIR-CUTTING AND DRESSING

Most refpectfully begs Leave to inform the NOBILITY, GENTRY, & LADIES of London
and the Home Counties that he fhall be attending thofe who may pleafe to honour him
with their commands during the prefent Race Week at the most famouf

VICKERY'S TEMPLE OF FASHION

The celebrity of Vickery's Shop is fo well known to the Fafhionable World, that it is unneceffary to
enlarge on the opportunities which J. KIRKLAND has had during the Years he has been there.
To prevent difappointment, application (naming the time and addrefs) are requefted to be made
as early as pofsible at Vickery's Temple of Fafhion, No. 6 Tavisftock-Street, Covent Garden.

'Thrilled beyond meafure! My daughter was perfonally coiffed by Mr. Kirkland, and
attending her firft Ball, was the toaft of the Town! Married her off within two months!'
Lady Georgiana Eliot

In a fuperior ftile of Tafte and Fafhion

My dear Cassandra, your letter is very concerning and I cannot but regret that you are so far from me. London is to my mind almost another more dangerous country and Bath by contrast so sedate. Can you not return sooner? The temptations offered by the Capital, and that of Mr Kirkland in particular, albeit with respectable connections to Vickery's Temple of Fashion, can serve no purpose other than to bring your character into disrepute. Only think of Mama's distress should you take up an offer from the above gentleman. He has no connections and no family of whom anyone has heard. I am so distracted that I have been unable to dress myself to walk even so far as Queen Square where I liked to sit with you by the Obelisk. Write by return and tell me that you will continue careful. It is to be supposed that your hairdresser cannot make you an offer until he has at least the promise of a higher situation. I have not the smallest hope of dissuading you if your mind is made up, unless to again underline the points I made in my last letter to you: be Prudent, Patient, Cool in your exchanges with this person upon whom you seem fixated, and Mindful of the little Family you will be leaving should you take the Fatal Course. The acquisition of an attendant coiffeur for us all would in no way mitigate the shock of marriage to a person of Trade.

How I wish that I were with you, dear, dearest, Cassandra so that we may walk and talk serenely together around the Circus. I assure you that your heart, although very sore at present, is still sound. There are other Mr Kirklands - and better - in this world with more honourable intentions involving marriage rather than elopement and disgrace. Think how impossible your prospects would have become had you agreed to this impetuous plan. You have too few clothes, only one spare chemise and one nightgown for your entire stay. You may think that your time would have been spent without need of any clothing at all at first - but money would have had eventually to be found to dress you. We will console one another for our single abandoned state and you will find, dearest one, that life will resume its old comfortable routine

ORIGINAL
TH OLIVER
THE BEDSIDE
Susan
Candy

Sister, As soon as you are here with us at No 25 we will take the precaution of calling upon Doctor Dimble so that he may ensure your good health and fully restore you to us. My Aunt tells us that you have lost all interest in sustaining yourself but we have no end of little milk dishes and your favourite Bath Olivers for your nourishment. Some fortifying wine of the blend that you enjoy will make you strong again. I have a mind to write to Mr Kirkland myself but Mama has disallowed this and declares that all connections between him and the Austen family must be severed. So mind that she does not learn if you fall into temptation and call him back to you. Of course, he may write to you himself and Mama will be certain to make it her business to prevent any letters reaching you (unread by her of course). Be of good cheer until your carriage reaches Gay Street after which you may feel free to release all your stifled feelings of despair and longing in the arms of your devoted sister.

Oh Cassie, I cannot find it in my heart to forgive Mama for keeping me here at home while you are sent away like a child to recover from your recent Disappointment. Were dear Papa still with us I believe that he would have wished us to remain together here or that we both should travel to Godmersham Park. We must be grateful that he will never know that you almost made the gravest of mistakes, poor dear foolish Sister. Upon your return to your familiar self we will take up our old habitual activities. Mama and I will be glad to have another pair of hands to help Biddy and Cook. Am I wrong to propose that you revert to your former way of life? You have tasted affection and I believe it may be hard for you. But I am here. Please be sure to remind Elizabeth to send the Brussels lace trim I asked for. You will see how it enhances the drawers and chemise I am at this moment cutting out ready.

To Cassandra's Rescue ~ The Kindly Knights of Bath
WISDOM AND WORLDLINESS
BY JANE [illegible]
GIN

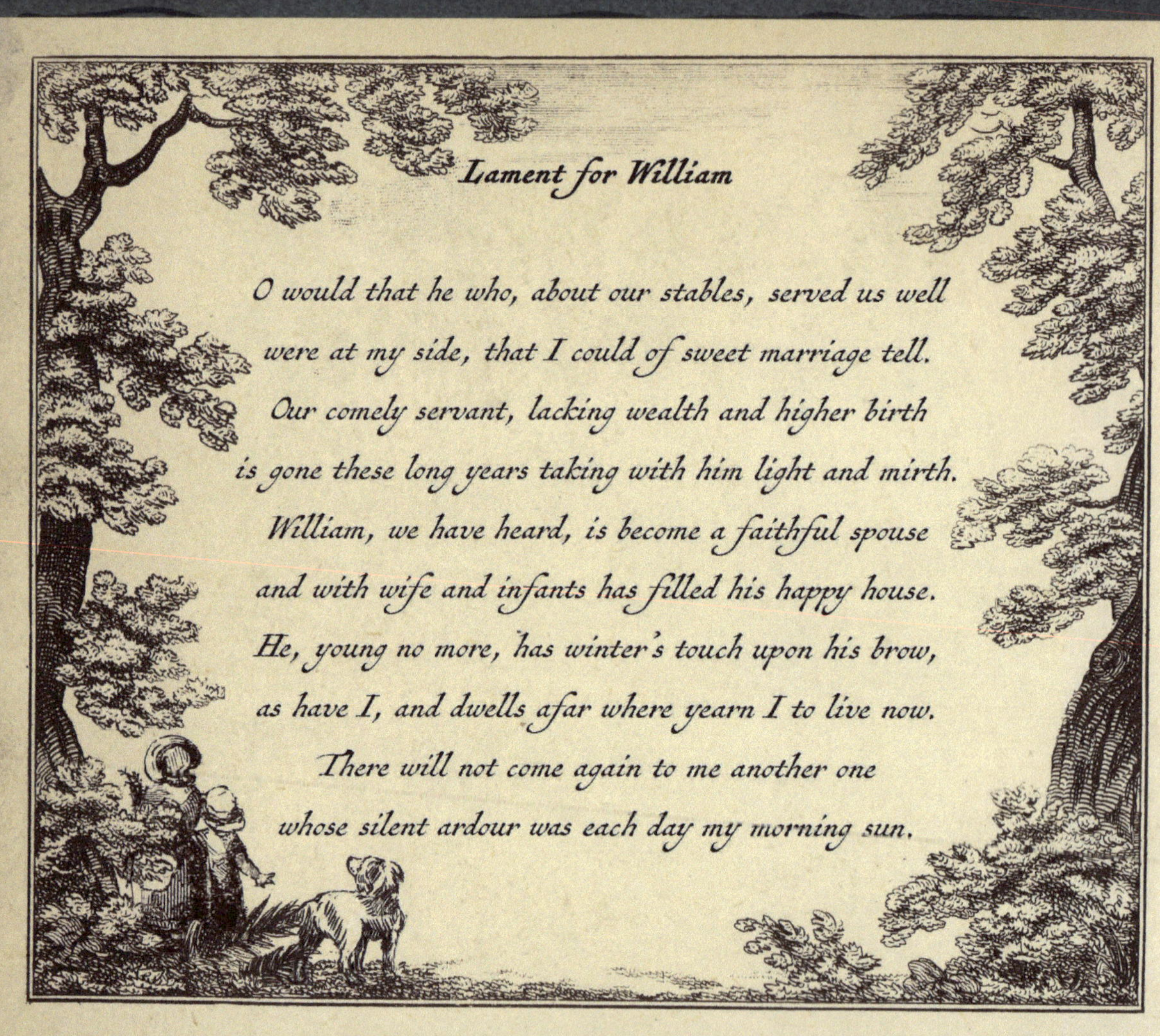

Lament for William

O would that he who, about our stables, served us well
were at my side, that I could of sweet marriage tell.
Our comely servant, lacking wealth and higher birth
is gone these long years taking with him light and mirth.
William, we have heard, is become a faithful spouse
and with wife and infants has filled his happy house.
He, young no more, has winter's touch upon his brow,
as have I, and dwells afar where yearn I to live now.
There will not come again to me another one
whose silent ardour was each day my morning sun.

Our sisterly attachment is all to me, my
dearest Cassandra, and looks likely to take first
place in my heart for the whole of our lives.
This does not however prevent longings,
especially at night, for another, whether of
that other sex or no, whose company would be
of a different kind: not sisterly but
understanding without speech every thought,
every craving. Can it be that such a one exists
— and that she is myself? No one understands
me better, no one admires my writing more. I
am my own perfect companion, a thought which
accompanies and comforts me.

CHRISTINE WEST

I began 'writing things down' at the age of five in an attempt to remember those things forever. I have never stopped. Although I was born and brought up in London I have lived in Cornwall for the greater part of my adult life with long interludes working in Switzerland and France. I translated a French Resistance member's long memoire, Drôle de Mère (An Odd Mother). In 2017 I wrote Days at Cnewr, the story of my husband Hugh West's wild childhood on a remote Welsh mountain farm. I worked for many years alongside my husband in our pottery but now I have hung up my apron to concentrate on writing novels, short stories, children's tales and poetry. My poems have appeared in British and American poetry reviews and anthologies.

LIZZIE NELSON

I am a British artist and author currently living in the suburbs of Chicago with my husband, daughter and dogs. I began writing after an arthritis diagnosis forced me to rethink painting murals and consider working small-scale and piling all my midlife bemusement and grumblings into humorous verse, poetry and illustration.

I published Fair to Piddling: A Journey Through Midlife in Humorous Verse, in 2020, followed by a collection of dog poetry, Doggy Biscuits, in 2022. I have illustrated for other authors, especially for children's books, including Uncle Bill's Missing Tooth by Grant Clark and, most recently, Dear Puppy by my friend and next door neighbour, Kelly Herda.

I produced a Jane Austen parody notebook, Writing With Jane, in 2021. It was filled with observations and tips presumably written by Jane and then mislaind for a couple of centuries. I met Christine through our dog accounts on Instagram. She kindly bought all my books and I began receiving mysterious letters from Jane Austen inspired by the quotes in Writing With Jane. Once I realized who they were from and how jolly good they were, Wisdom and Worldliness was born. I may be found on social media as @thedogpoet and @fairtomiddlingmidlifehumor. And if you love Jane Austen as much as we do, follow us @ohjane.austen on Instagram.

Fair to Piddling is a collection of illustrated humorous light verse. Charting my own journey from thirties to fifties, you may find much that resonates and even more to chuckle about.

'We Loved This!!! Witty, funny and thought provoking.'
Mark Adderley and Nadia Sawalha

'Fantastic!! Absolutely fantastic, laugh out loud on every page. You will find yourself singing, laughing and laughing some more. Light hearted, highly recommend.'
The Menopause Queen

I·thoroughly enjoyed it, read it three times straight off. Sent it to my menopausal daughter but told her I wanted it back!
Beryl Cross aged 90

Doggy Biscuits is a humorous, entertaining and brilliantly observed collection of poetry and words inspired by rescue pups, Max and Griffin. Mostly reviewed by dogs:

'Gots our copy of Doggy Biscuits yesterday and Mum has already read it cover to cover. Hers incessant chuckling is drivings me crazy. Thanks a lot @thedogpoet! Mum says dis book is a must haves for all pupper owners.'
Simon_von_schnauzer

'I loved these poems. It's just a shame they were all about dogs.'
Henry (Brian Bilston's Cat)

'A fun read for poetry-loving dog people! Packed with humorous verse and adorable dog photos.'
Modern Dog Magazine

You may find my website, more books and all sorts of art and cards via my QR code or link below:

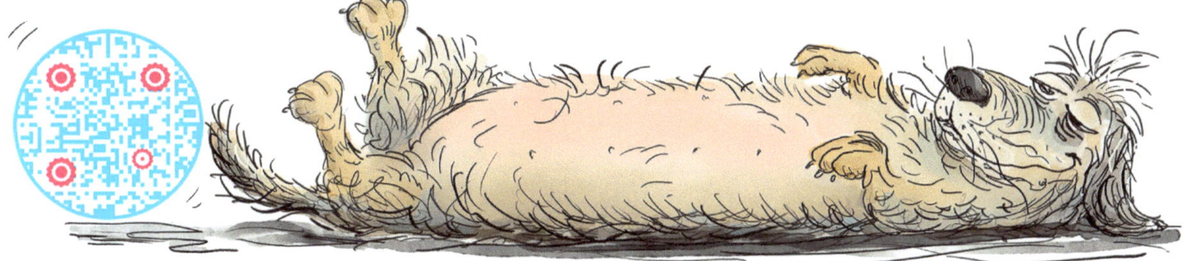

https://linktr.ee/lizzienelson

AIDE-MÉMOIRE

While writing by the window, do not allow your eyes to linger on the young groom for very long.
Well, just a bit then!